ALL WOMEN IN ONE

ALL WOMEN IN ONE

DEJAN STOJANOVIĆ

New Avenue Books

New Avenue Books

First Edition

Library of Congress Control Number: 2025934784

ISBN-13: 978-1-966571-18-6

NOTE TO THIS EDITION

The poems in this collection are part of a series titled *The Embrace of Light and Darkness,* marking their first publication in book form. The collection includes poems originally written in English between 2005 and 2010, with a few exceptions added or fixed later.

D. S.

Contents

ALL WOMEN IN ONE...i

NOTE TO THIS EDITION v

I SMELL YOU EVERYWHERE..9

GARDEN OF LIGHT 11

A WOMAN IN THE GARDEN OF LIGHT 13

ALL WOMEN IN ONE..14

POETRY AND WOMEN..15

LOVE IN ARIZONA 17

RAIN 18

MORNING 19

THE ART OF LOVE...20

MUSES 23

MUSE I 25

MUSE II 26

BIRTHPLACE...27

HARBOR..28

II 29

LIFE...30

BECOMING ONE...31

THE SAME STORY 33

FANTASY 34

THE TOP 35

SIRENS...37

YOU DON'T NEED TO SAY ANYTHING 39

A NIGHT WORTH A LIFE 40

SPECIAL FEELING 41

UNSAID DELIGHT..43

EARLY MORNING...45

STAYING CRAZY 46

YOU ARE THE STAR..48

TWO STARS 50

SIREN 51

DREAMS 53

DON QUIXOTE 55

THE WORLD 58

WE COME FROM THE SAME PLACE.................... 59

HEART 60

DON JUAN 61

LOVER 62

LIVE TO LOVE... 63

RECIPE FOR LOVE 64

ARMOR OF LOVE 65

CHANCES 67

FIRST LOVE 69

MOMENTS WORTH THE WHOLE ETERNITY 70

PATH 72

THE HEALING POWER OF A KISS 73

FUN... 74

WORDS AND LEAVES.. 75

UNFORESEEN MOMENT 76

BREAK UP 77

THE LILAC LAND 79

LILAC WORLD 81

WORDS, MUSIC, AND LIGHT 83

II... 84

III.. 85

IV 87

V... 88

ABOUT THE AUTHOR.. 89

I SMELL YOU EVERYWHERE

The world blooms,
Words bloom;
Scents fill the air.

I see you blossoming,
Hear your winged words,
And smell you everywhere.

GARDEN OF LIGHT

A WOMAN IN THE GARDEN OF LIGHT

Longing to explore a hidden, sacred place,

I break through obstacles

To recognize the invisible sparks

Emanating from the precious discovery

Of the space between us,

Shining solely with longing.

I witness the awakening stars,

The birth of new landscapes,

Future cities, and temples,

I hear new stories falling

From the fountains of hidden art,

Where all the old sounds and colors

Transform into stars in the Garden.

And you—blindingly bright—

Melt me into new sensations

As I grow into the core,

With invisible roots that pierce,

Touching the essence of fire.
I traveled far to that place before space and time,
And return to this Garden to find you,
To see the real you, swimming
And flying ahead of the light
To discover you where the light never was
To learn that you are its source.

ALL WOMEN IN ONE

You shall not stop or hesitate
Until you pass through the forest,
And compare the beauty of day and night in summer—
Until you arrive in your own Ithaca.

There is always Venus,
A new Elissa to build a new Carthage,
A new Kingdom of Light.

You shall not stop until you find Venus:
One woman in all,
And all women in one.

Until you can say—*La Dolce Vita*,
Until you discover *Paradise Lost* in just one name,
Until you can say—
You are all women in one.

POETRY AND WOMEN

We no longer need to pray for rain,
Or petition the sky for more wheat, sugar, flour, and flowers.
We don't need to go to the Oracle of Delphi
Or seek to name new gods.

Yet, we still feel what our ancestors felt,
We still gaze at the same sky,
Smile at the same stars,
And listen to the same sea.

The essence of a woman has never changed.
Her role has shifted through different eras,
But a woman remains what she has always been—
Man's glory, destination, and dream.

As long as a woman breathes,
We will sing and send prayers to the gods and goddesses.
As long as she shines in our dreams,
We will listen to the winds carrying news on their lips.

We have attracted even more rain than we needed,
Creating and dismantling our gods.
We have sent our prayers to both old and new deities,

Born pagans, then baptized.

We have witnessed change—
Countries disappearing and new ones being born.
We have seen all metamorphoses, but not in her.
The song will never die.

You are a vestal virgin and a courtesan,
A famous star and a wild animal,
A reminder of bliss and a puzzle;
Nobody can tame you, only attain through fight.

You are Delilah and Judith,
A proud and dangerous black widow.
You are the industrious Elissa,
Waving from the shores of Carthage.

It must be that another
Has caught the vigor of Dido,
Heard her voice, and saw her silhouette in the blue
Beam over the sea, in the Mediterranean light.

(Godot is always waiting.
He is probably waiting for a woman.)

LOVE IN ARIZONA

You are from California,
I am from the Midwest,
But we met in Arizona
And went to the desert
To measure the thorns
Of the lonely, scattered cacti.
We measured the light rays,
Measured the distance
Between us and the world,
Measured the love, kisses, and screams
In the solemn silence of the desert.

We kissed the dusty ground
And asked the dry land for a reason,
But the ground was silent,
And we fell silent, too.
There was no measure, no reason,
Only life, only life
In the desolate desert.
And we kissed more
And did not ask for a reason
Anymore.

RAIN

Those who hate rain hate life.
Nothing reminds us of awakening quite like rain.

We listen to the drops falling
Over the forests, over the rooftops,
Over the streets, and us
As we dream of another unforgettable night
Like this one, which is unrepeatable.
Our emotions flow into the rainy streets,
Soaking the ground even more
With our rainy thoughts and feelings.

As we soar high, we become clouds,
Transforming into drops
That fall over rooftops and streets,
Becoming rain and embracing this feeling.
Little do we know that the rain teaches us
What it means to be alive:
Not knowing, yet still discovering
More than knowledge can ever convey.

Nothing reminds us of awakening quite like rain,
And so we await the sunlight.

MORNING

He placed a rose on the bedside table
While she was still sleeping.
His wake-up message rested on the stand—
Her smile reflected on his face
Filling him with bliss.

Remembrance—
The memory box opens.
Anticipation—
The future is revealed and embraced.

Back and forth,
Through memories and experiences,
She recognizes this morning
In her awakened spirit.

She notices the mist,
The rose, the dewy grass;
She sees his enlightened face
And steps into the new morning with a smile.

THE ART OF LOVE

It was then,

When the breeze tousled your hair,

When you hadn't thought about styling,

Yet were always stylish in your natural grace.

You discovered the source of attraction,

Unaware of the hidden power

Radiating from your face.

You walked confidently

Through the streets of Kotor.

It was then,

When you felt the importance of art,

And realized that without art,

Even love cannot survive—

Love is a unique science.

It was then,

Under the birch tree,

When you felt the breeze

Whispering in your ears,

Conveying untranslatable meanings

That you understood without prior knowledge.

It was then

That you became an artist.

TELL ME EVERYTHING

Sing to me of the times when you first saw the Moon,
When you felt a deep connection with the World,
Understanding more by knowing less,
When you sensed the pulse of the entire family
Hanging in the unknown;
Of the moments when your feelings were innocent;
When a single glance conveyed more than words.

Sing to me about the formation of flowers,
About the shapes of invisible things—
Colors in other dimensions,
About secret formulas;
About feelings you never express in words.

You dream of my life.
I am living your dream—
Writing your book.

Sing to me.

MUSES

MUSE I

Recognize your Muse
Among the multitude of whispers

To see her shining through many colors,
Tune your senses.
Listen to the highest tones.

Fly beyond the scale
To hear her melody,
Adjust your ears and eyes

To colors beyond the spectrum,
Recognize her beyond just yellow and blue,
Creating your own rainbow.

Find a way to connect with her,
Capturing her grace in the sublime
So that the Muse can recognize you

Among the multitudes.
Whisper back to her, using newly invented notes.
Show her the new colors of the rainbow.

MUSE II

Invite me to your Castle;
Arm me with your secret weapons,

To know that I know
What I feel is true;
To know that I feel
What I know is true.

To learn how to lose my senses,
I must make use of the expanding universe
To grow in every direction,
Dream with open eyes and see in the darkness.

I am, and I am not;
You shape me.
You are, and you are not;
We don't truly exist unless we recognize each other.

BIRTHPLACE

My dream is your birthplace;
Your presence is my life.

I follow your spells,
Listen to your songs—
They cure my madness.

You are my savior,
Sending light ahead
So the dream can continue to dream.

Your whispers await me
In every city and street.
The light sings your song.

You save me from myself
During my wanderings.
Those whispers become amulets,

And I keep walking
To keep you alive.

HARBOR

I

I will find you when I least expect it.
You are my Road.

Roads travel through us,
Never arriving at a harbor.

We are both travelers and roads.
All lovers are wanderers.

Our journey is our Road;
Our wanderings are the harbor.

II

You are the Dream,
And I dream of you.

You are the beginning
And the Harbor.

I dream of the world,
And you are the World.

You are here, and you disappear,
Yet you never truly leave me.

You bloom from my heart.
If I lose you, you find me.

If you forget me, I remind you
To dream for me.

If you lose me, I find you
To keep me dreaming.

LIFE

Entering the matter,
You recreate our biology,
Merging with my atoms,
Passing through them like invisible light,

Two swallowing forces—
Not only partners,
But two harmonious songs
Creating new substances.

I am your reason for seeing.
You are my reason for shining.
I am your singer;
You are my song.

You are my ears;
I am your voice.
You are my passion;
I am your measure.

You are my wings;
I am your flight.
You are my life;
I am your dream.

BECOMING ONE

Tell me my story,
And I will tell you yours.

Breathe my air,
And I will be your eyes.

I will hear your whispers
When you translate my touch.

You help me walk,
And I will help you fly.

We will fly and sing,
Circle and fall.

To lift us higher again,
We catch the whispers of flight.

We follow racing words,
Chasing them together.

We see them screaming and making love,
Learning the deepest secrets.

The secret of silence
Draws us into a deep stillness,

Needing nothing—
Not even a word.

THE SAME STORY

Thousands of years old, this story
Tells the same tale we hear today.

We search for new words
To offer new meanings

To old feelings,
Evolving from different sounds

Across time and space
In new landscapes

Where roses smell stronger,
And feelings do not require words.

FANTASY

Life is our fantasy.
We are the actors.

Do we act out life,
Or is life the only true actor?

Do we play our roles,
Or do we attempt to deceive
The greatest Deceiver of all?

Life is the greatest Deceiver's fantasy,
And we are merely actors in his play.

So why do we fantasize about the fantasy?
True fantasy does not require acting.

We shall live it.

THE TOP

I chase you.
You hide—
Then you appear and wave to me.

I chase you again,
Find you by chance,
Then you disappear.

You hit me from behind—
I turn around,
And you are not there.

I chase you once more.
You jump behind the hill
And see me on the peak.

You run into the forest,
Circling and screaming,
Dangerously dancing toward the top.

Then you stop and wait for me—
You kiss me and run away;
The chase doesn't end.

Faster and faster you run;
My legs cannot keep up.
You wear me down.

Then you appear at the top,
Waving to me to join you
So, I slowly step to the top.

"This is where we belong," you said,
And I felt the whole mountain
Tremble for a moment as we hugged.

SIRENS

YOU DON'T NEED TO SAY ANYTHING

What more can we say about voyages,
About the seas, love, loneliness,
Gentle thoughts, tears, and laughter—
What more is there to uncover
About the secrets of the world?

You don't need to say anything;
You need to be, see, and feel—not tell.
The best stories often remain unspoken.
Listening to the sea can open pathways
To the great source of light within you,
As you search for it outside.

For the voyage, you need nothing more
Than a desire to inhale the world.

A NIGHT WORTH A LIFE

I see you anew tonight.
Thoughts on fire,
They burn and scream—
You are new tonight.

Reborn from the fire,
I become a flame,
Burning in bliss
For this brief night.

SPECIAL FEELING

To feel without understanding
And to understand through feeling;
To express it without words
And know it before knowing.

To be silently eloquent
And inquire without asking a question,
To receive the answer nonetheless
And acknowledge it with a smile.

To recognize it through a smile
And express it in silence,
To convey it without actually saying—
That's when you truly understand.

To feel is to know;
Not naming it is to honor it—
To do it for a smile
And not seek any other reward.

To walk, dance, and fly,
Embrace the epiphany of oblivion;
To be one with the world

And live to feel it.

That's when you truly understand it.

UNSAID DELIGHT

What I can say,
And what I cannot say—
It is not just a word,
But an unsaid delight.

What I can sing,
Or only dream—
It is not merely a note,
But an unwritten song.

What I can know
But not express,
Or can express but not fully understand—
It is the moment of greatest intensity.

What I dream,
And do not live—
Or live without dreaming,
Becomes a bad dream.

What I remember,
And what I forget—
It is not merely a memory

But the soul's selective sanctuary.

What I know,
And what I feel,
Even if I can express it in words—
It is a vast unwritten world.

EARLY MORNING

We left early that morning to ride horses,

Feel the fresh air, and see the Sun.

We planned to explore the forest

And rest on a blanket when we grew tired of riding.

We witnessed the red sky

And saw the Sun rising over the forest,

Taking in the refreshing air

In that still, dreamy world.

STAYING CRAZY

I promised to write you a poem
Every day for a year.
Each day, a new flower.
I promised to write flowers for you.

I promised to share a fairy tale
Every day for a year.
I promised something new
And vowed to collect it.

I promised to lift you up—
You were afraid you might fall.
I pledged my words to your throne
To keep the foundation strong.

I promised to write your memory
And rewrite your thoughts.
I promised not to let you fall,
For my words support the throne.

And after every promise delivered,
We became crazier and couldn't believe
How easy it was to keep promises

And how simple it is to be crazy.

As every word became a bird,
And every word blossomed into a flower,
We realized how wonderful it is to be crazy—
And you embraced my madness.

Your fears had no foundation.
You felt comfortable
In your magnificent role.
We promised we would never stop.

We promised never to stop writing poems,
We promised to keep the words soaring,
We promised to keep the throne fresh and alive,
We promised to stay crazy.

YOU ARE THE STAR

Every journey is as ancient and long
As the journey of a star.
You are made of stardust.

Remember your old home,
Your innate glory,
Long travels you've experienced.

There is no place too dark
That cannot be illuminated.
No darkness is stronger than light.

And if you forget—
Or when you forget—
Try to dream and remember.

And if you fall—
Or when you fall—
Remember your home of light.

And if you can't find your way,
Or if you are lost in the jungle,
Look up at the sky.

The sky will guide you on your path.

STAR

Far yet always present,
You were waiting to be born.

From a dream long ago, you emerged,
Waiting to be seen.

Sensed by many but never truly noticed,
Your silent words are understood yet heard by no one.

You touched others, but no one touched you;
You felt sensations while they were asleep.

You needed to be found,
Reborn in an intentional accident.

Though being light, you still needed light,
But no one was a star.

A star needs a star.

TWO STARS

That evening, still alive,
We asked the sea about its secrets
And were surprised it did not hear us,
Or perhaps it was just pretending.

Mediterranean miracles,
The waves of the Adriatic Sea,
Cypresses and mimosas,
Crying insects and fireflies.

Soft like the Mediterranean Sea,
You carried the scent of summer.
You—that evening still alive,
That sea I still see.

The stars were too far and silent.
We screamed to get closer to them,
To break the silence,
To make them hear us.

We were the two loudest creatures
On the entire Mediterranean;
We screamed louder than all the insects and birds,
Imagining we were two stars.

SIREN

From the sea, she sings her seductive song;
Even Odysseus cannot escape it.

Even he falls into her net.
Every man dreams of being ensnared
By a Siren and hearing her song
At least once.

To be captivated
By the enchanting sound of the sea,
And to dream of how to escape
And return to solid ground.

A man proves his courage on the open sea,
Where only the sea measures the sky,
And the sky reflects the sea,
When days are long and nights echo the Siren's song

Of voyages to distant shores,
Every wave hides the secret,
Decodable only through a long friendship with the sky.
Siren was born out of this love.

Every man needs his Siren

To check his courage and strength

When he hears her song

In his travels through the unknown.

DREAMS

DON QUIXOTE

We dream and fight
With demons, both real and imagined
We truly live only when we dream;
We grow from our dreams,

From our own La Mancha.
Don Quixote is not merely an imaginary figure;
He is as real as Alexander the Great,
His Dulcinea is as real as Cleopatra.

His windmills are as real as the Library of Alexandria;
As real as the many languages that are now dead and forgotten;
As real as Attila or the loss of Constantinople.
His windmills represent lost Ayah Sofias,

His battles had to be fought
By sleepy emperors
Too preoccupied to engage in them.
We need Don Quixote and La Mancha

For when the whole past feels like a phantom,
When many cities have fallen,
The idea remains—

Stronger than any city, stronger than any empire.

Quixote shines through Lorca and Picasso;
From Dalí and El Greco;
From the gloomy *View of Toledo.*
He was born before Cervantes.

Those in Argentina, Mexico, and Peru,
Colombia and the Caribbean
Carry La Mancha and Quixote in their hearts,
For he is an ultimate and often overlooked Don Juan.

Garcia Márquez was not born in Colombia.
He was born in Macondo,
And his Macondo is his La Mancha.
Fuentes and Cortázar are from La Mancha, too.

Neruda had his first dream,
First meeting with the Moon and the Sun,
In sunny La Mancha, hiding in his heart,
Where he learned how to sing like a nightingale.

Don Quixote is not just Don Quixote;
La Mancha is not just geography.
It is our inner territory—
Terra Nostra.

It does not matter what happens where,

Where we fall or rise,

What we conquer or lose,

How big or small we are.

All places come and go.

History will be erased in the universal purgatory.

Dreams are our only geography—

Our native land.

THE WORLD

Fight against those who oppose beauty,
And share what you observe
When you interpret the words of light—
The essence of all worlds.

The same story exists across all worlds,
Yet each world is distinct,
Just as every word offers new meaning
To the universal Source of Everything.

WE COME FROM THE SAME PLACE

You say we come from the same place.

You claim that you have lived within me since we parted ways

And that I have lived within you.

We are each other's home, and that is where we belong.

HEART

Deceived by feelings and misled by knowledge—
You should turn to the heart,
Or allow the mind to calculate and deceive you even further.

Do you hear the music of the heart when you listen to it?
Let it guide your choices, and do not regret it.

DON JUAN

The most charming psychopath in history,
Whether real or imagined,
Played with the dreams of women
Who believed he would be gentle
And wouldn't betray love.

By recognizing their dreams,
He seduced them into the game
Of playing out their own stories,
Uncovering the secrets of their hearts
In the seductive hell of deceit.

LOVER

There is no born lover,
For we are all lovers

Although some are in a state of amnesia,
Overlooking the light of a sleeping star.

To dream occasionally is not dreaming
To love occasionally is not love.

There is always a dreaming star
Hiding within you, waiting to shine.

LIVE TO LOVE

To truly live,
To live for love,
To love for love,
To be alive,

We don't need devices
As much as we need scents.
We don't need more air
As much as we need new wings.

We don't need new elements—
We need refreshment.
Nothing is ever new;
It is only a discovery.

We need to desire to fly,
To fly to live,
To fly to love,
To love flying and to live flying.

RECIPE FOR LOVE

If someone needs lessons in love,
They may already be lost.
From ashes, you cannot ignite a fire;
Perhaps they are souls that have already burned out.

But, maybe they can learn how not to hate—
How to appreciate the closeness
Of someone who does not require a teacher,
And how to understand rather than just learn.

It's as simple as walking, talking, eating, or breathing,
Yet for some people, it seems harder than building a house.
However, what is the value of a house
Without these invisible ingredients built into it?

ARMOR OF LOVE

Love will save you from despair,

Of a certain death—

Death cannot outsmart love.

It is your armor,

Protecting you from the tricks of life.

CHANCES

FIRST LOVE

Forgotten feelings and words,
Or are we simply asleep?

Shy to feel or too weak to name it,
Afraid of losing or being lost and frozen

In a hug, while the music played,
On the terrace in St. Stefan

When we first felt it
And watched the mischievous waves

Drumming like a pendulum
Against the shore.

MOMENTS WORTH THE WHOLE ETERNITY

They happen anytime,
In any place,
In ways we don't understand.
We only know they are true.

When we ask for a reason,
We know they are not real.
When we cannot find the answer,
We know they are true.

We see more light,
Becoming lighter,
Knowing they are
Moments worth an eternity.

I throw a little dagger;
It flies back to me
And wounds me more deeply.
That is the price we pay.

When we say hello,
It is done with a smile,
And when we say goodbye,
It is with a kiss.

FLOWER

You are more than you realize.
A flower doesn't recognize its fragrance.

The One who unfolds your petals
Holds the key to your soul.

From the shimmering source, you shine from within,
And deep inside, he senses that source.

PATH

You either find the Path,
Or the Path finds you.

If the Path makes a choice,
You will become the light.

When there is no light,
You will still see.

When the light is too bright,
You will not be blinded.

You will be neither lost in darkness
Nor seduced by glory.

The light is your birthplace;
Life is your Path.

THE HEALING POWER OF A KISS

A kiss in the morning
Is enough to start the day.

A kiss at dawn
Is enough to begin a whole life.

A kiss in every place—
Under the tree, on the sidewalk,

On the bridge, and along both shores.
In our wanderings, it serves as a talisman.

A kiss in your memory is an instant delight
When you feel sad and alone.

FUN

Tell me a joke so we can laugh together.
We might even defy the law of gravity
By creating a new law of gravity
Filled with joy and adventure,
Ensuring lifelong fun.

WORDS AND LEAVES

Words and music fill the air—
Leaves dance on a windy day,
Waiting for a passerby,
A fleeting moment to embrace
And catch its melody,
Fading slowly into oblivion.

UNFORESEEN MOMENT

Something always lingers,

Forgotten deeply and unresolved,

Waiting to return at an unforeseen moment,

Reminding us to accept it as due.

BREAK UP

It ended.
Just like that—
Quick,
No explanation.

Are all problems so simple?
Or do they linger, dying a slow, overdue death
Under the weight of reasoning?

With poor explanations,
Poor judgments,
And poorer decisions.

It is better this way—
Quick,
As sharp as a knife.
A new opportunity

For life awaits
For another chance,
And for you.

THE LILAC LAND

LILAC WORLD

Words have their own fragrances,

And can transform the world into a garden of flowers.

Every petal carries a new word, a new scent.

The world becomes a giant lilac.

"Breathe me," I say.

We have been waiting for a long time,

Both in a rush and at leisure.

Amid the turmoil, you whispered,

"You might miss your chances."

You reminded me

That we should not pursue every opportunity before us;

An obvious opportunity can be a distraction,

Preventing us from seeing the bigger chance ahead.

You taught me that

Sometimes, the best opportunities are the ones we choose not to act

    upon.

The greatest successes can come unexpectedly,

And the best chances arise from patience.

Neither of us hit the first ball.

Neither of us seized every opportunity.

Our score reflects the missed opportunities and chances.

We chose not to take every chance

By refraining from pursuing every opportunity that came our way.

The breeze carries our whispers

As we dance and savor them under the starry sky

In the lilac world, where we arrived by passing up another chance.

WORDS, MUSIC, AND LIGHT
I

Words cannot heal the deep wounds caused by impatience.

Healing comes from understanding those wounds,
Rooted in the pain of birth and the struggles of growth.

Words become ineffective when perspective is limited.
They cannot mend a soul another has hurt,

Nor can they bridge the gap
Created by unseen vistas and unheard sounds.

Everything is a word, but it is more than just a word.
Light sings, and music shines.

II

Words are sources of both sorrow and joy,
Soft and sharp, like swords,
Carrying fragrances
Filled with the sounds of singing birds,
Whispers, and flowing rivers.
The world emerges from words.

Words guide our roles and actions.
We strive to conquer and enchant one another
To win the ultimate game,
Navigating unpredictable paths,
Becoming both servants and rulers.

Yet, we drift apart.
Countless words build walls between us,
Sucking up the air and destroying bridges,
Leaving no room for movement;
No space for words,
And no chance to mend anything.

All words can be lethal—both soft and sharp;
To soothe our pride, we let them take control.
Excessive knowledge can extinguish love,
As we learn to live beyond words and grow from silence.

III

Words are flying
From the leaves,
And we are trying to catch them.

You are soaring with them,
Catching them mid-flight
And bringing them to me.

You attempt to build a garden,
Enchanting whispers
Singing about the journey.

Every lily holds your secret:
A new whisper, a new word, a new flower.
We are getting closer to the Garden.

Nobody knows
About our secret palace;
Nobody senses its existence.

I am landing in your Garden,
You take me by the hand,
Turning another page into a lily.

The scents are flowing;
Every page reveals a new flower.
I am moving through your Castle.

Every room holds a new word,
New flowers blooming,
New whispers and scents.

I am moving through your Castle,
Where every sound sings,
And every word has a smell.

Then, I find the most comfortable corner
Of your Castle and lie on your pillows,
Feeling your touch.

And you move into my heart,
Savoring my words.
"This is your Castle," you say.

IV

Letters grow on the trees,
Rivers flow towards us.
The world expands from us.
We hear more and say less,
Or speak only what we must.
We need no measurements
For actions that seek no recognition.
The world is clear, and we are clear.

V

You give life to my words

That brush against me through your lips,

And my lips echo your kisses.

We understand our silence,

And we deserve it.

ABOUT THE AUTHOR

Dejan Stojanović (1959) was born in Peć, Kosovo (formerly part of Serbia, Yugoslavia). Although he received a legal education, he has never practiced law. Instead, he became a journalist and foreign correspondent in the early 1990s; however, he is primarily a poet, essayist, philosopher, and businessman.

He has published the following poetry collections:

Circling (Krugovanje), Narodna knjiga—Alfa, Belgrade, published in three editions: 1993, 1998, and 2000.
The Sun Watches Itself (Sunce sebe gleda), NIP Književna reč, Belgrade, 1999.
The Sign and Its Children (Znak i njegova deca), Prosveta, Belgrade, 2000.
The Creator (Tvoritelj), Narodna knjiga, Belgrade, 2000.
The Shape (Oblik), Gramatik, Podgorica, 2000.
The Dance of Time (Ples vremena), Konras, Belgrade, 2007.

Pentalogy: *The World in Nowherness (Svet u nigdini),* Udruženje književnika Srbije, Belgrade, 2017:
(1) *Ozar (Ozar),*
(2) *The World and God (Svet i Bog),*
(3) *The World in Nowhereness (Svet u nigdini),*
(4) *The World and Humans (Svet i ljudi),*
(5) *The Home of Light (Dom svetlosti).*

The Hidden Light (Skrivena svetlost), Čigoja, Belgrade, 2018.
Primordial Spark (Iskra iskona), Albatros plus, Belgrade, 2021.
Centuries and Steps (Vekovi i koraci), Albatros plus, Belgrade, 2023.

Essays:

Creator and Creating (Stvaralac i stvaranje), Albatros plus, Belgrade, 2021.

The New Man and the New World (Novočovek i novosvet), Rad, Belgrade, 2022.

Anthology: *Selected Serbian Plays* (*Izabrane srpske drame*), USA, 2016.

A book of his selected interviews, *Conversations* (*Razgovori*), was published in 1999 by NIP Književna reč in Belgrade. The Serbian Heritage Foundation and the Association of Writers of Serbia for Intellectual Engagement awarded the book the Rastko Petrović Prize.

Collected Poems: 1978-2000 (Pentalogy 1), New Avenue Books, 2025 (Translation from Serbian).

Books written in English:

Philosophy: *Absolute,* New Avenue Books, USA, 2024.

Poetry Series: *The Embrace of Light and Darkness* (Pentalogy 3):
- *Dance of Sounds*, New Avenue Books, 2025
- *The Matter of Matter*, New Avenue Books, 2025
- *The Home of the World*, New Avenue Books, 2025
- *All Women in One*, New Avenue Books, 2025
- *Strange Thoughts* (prose), New Avenue Books, 2025

He lived in Chicago, USA, from 1990 to 2014, and holds citizenship in both Serbia and the United States.

www.ingramcontent.com/pod-product-compliance
Lightning Source LLC
Chambersburg PA
CBHW052014240626

47153CB00008B/2868